Not Blessed

Harold Abramowitz

with an Introduction by
Teresa Carmody

TRENCHART: Maneuvers Series

𝅗𝅥

LES FIGUES PRESS
Los Angeles

Not Blessed
FIRST EDITION

ISBN 10: 1-934254-13-4
ISBN 13: 978-1-934254-13-4

Library of Congress Control Number: 2010922600

Les Figues Press thanks its members for their support and readership. Les
Figues Press is a 501(c)3 organization. Donations are tax-deductible.

This project is supported in part by generous grants from the Los
Angeles County Board of Supervisors through the Los Angeles
County Arts Commission and from the National Endowment of
the Arts.

The author would like to gratefully acknowledge the following
individuals: Teresa Carmody, Vanessa Place, and Christine
Wertheim.

Les Figues would like to acknowledge the following individuals
for their generosity: Johanna Blakley and Peter Binkow, Diane and
Chris Calkins, and Coco Owen. Special thanks also to Vanessa
Place, Erin Bower, Jennifer Calkins, Vincent Dachy, Elizabeth Hall,
and Pam Ore.

Distributed by SPD / Small Press Distribution
1341 Seventh Street
Berkeley, CA 94710
www.spdbooks.org

TrenchArt 5/2
Book 3 of 5 in the TRENCHART Maneuvers Series.

LES FIGUES PRESS
Post Office Box 7736
Los Angeles, CA 90007
323.734.4732 / info@lesfigues.com
www.lesfigues.com
www.lesfigues.blogspot.com

To Sharone and Karena

Introduction

Not Blessed is a piece of propaganda. It will convince you of certain things. Strange, uncanny feelings like déjà vu, for example, or deliberate compulsiveness as a characteristic within select modern texts.

Not Blessed is an answer to an unarticulated question. This question may be, "How can one affect certain thoughts and feelings in the hearts and minds of others?" This is not an unusual question in general, and in the literary arts it is so ordinary a question that it is implied within all works of literature. To this end, a writer may use point-of-view, voice and tone, rhyme, alliteration and prosody, to name just a few of the many elements which work together to create the total effect of a piece. In *Not Blessed*, Harold Abramowitz keeps the sentences mostly short and declarative. He punctuates dependent clauses as if they are fully sound, and makes excellent use of large and small repetitions. There are shifts in tense and point-of-view. Each of these contributes, piece by piece, bit by bit, to the unsettling yet quietly authoritative affect of *Not Blessed*.

Like literature, propaganda also aims to influence others' attitudes, generally toward a specific cause or position, more or less directly political, frequently commercial. Propaganda techniques include tireless repetition of a point, the creation or deletion of information, half-truths, including improper punctuation and double-meanings, oversimplification, rationalization through vague and pleasant phrases and scapegoating. Abramowitz uses each of these and more in *Not Blessed*, which is, after all, a work of fiction. This raises another unstated question: what is the difference between literature and propaganda? Well, you might say, propaganda directs the audience—*Have it Your Way!*—to a predetermined conclusion—*Coke is It!*—while literature, in the best sense of the word, directs an audience to pause and reconsider. In other words, propaganda tells you what to think, while literature says think![1] What then to make of *Not Blessed*, which uses the tricks and techniques of propaganda to say, at least in part, *Dear reader, Think!*

"In answer to your question, I will tell you a little story," (5) says the narrator(s) of *Not Blessed*, thus avoiding a direct response. He proceeds to tell the story not once but twenty-eight times, one time per each of the book's twenty-eight[2] sections. Yet

[1] Of course, by this definition any number of books currently classified as literature more properly belong on the shelf labeled propaganda.

[2] Twenty-eight because Abramowitz initially drafted the text on twenty-eight consecutive days in February.

he never tells the same story twice, for in each telling, the story shifts. Clearly, Abramowitz deliberately chose this story (or more precisely, the story's principle characters and events) as a narrative constraint, yet once chosen, the constraint acts as a compulsion within the text. The story becomes a landing point the narrator *must* reach in every section, yet the more times the story is told, the less necessary its exact details become. The story's principles begin to work a spell of compulsive sense-making on the reader, so even when the sentences begin to do strange, unlawful things, the characters and events still *make sense.*

This is not the only contradiction in *Not Blessed.* "There are, in fact, no constraints here," claims the narrator, "and there is nothing more than meaninglessness" (7). Why would the narrator claim the absence of a constraint so obvious as the repeating story motif unless: a) the narrator is acknowledging, indirectly, his own unreliability; b) the story's repetition does not meet the strict definition of "constraint" as defined by leading authorities; or c) this is yet another line of deliberately misleading propaganda. There isn't one apparent answer, and the claim of meaninglessness is likewise specious: if this story truly doesn't mean anything, why does the narrator keep compulsively remembering it? And what of its archetypical qualities—a boy, a grandmother, a policeman, the woods, a road with its parallel other. There is also the contradictory title, for *blessed* is a word with generally positive connotations, a positiveness which isn't negated by mere use of the word *not*. To be not blessed is not nearly as damning as being cursed, though the curse follows close behind, as noted in the book's epigraph from Jeremiah.

I read *Not Blessed* while sitting at the Starbucks in Valencia, California, which looked like so many Starbucks all over the world: the workers wore the same dark green aprons while standing behind the same stone-style counter, next to the same arched glass display case filled with baked goods, all the same. I read *Not Blessed* and listened to a woman with light colored hair (like mine!) tell another woman why Protestantism is better than Catholicism (an argument I used to make!). I could tell you a story to explain why I was sitting at the corporate coffee shop instead of a local, independent, or why, in my youth, I was such a zealous proselytizer of not just Protestantism, but of a particularly fundamentalist brand. I could tell you story after story about my good intentions and formative years, with charm and by way of justification, but the fact of my actions would remain emphasized, rather than dispelled, by the retelling. A retelling, after all, which might shift over the years. I read *Not Blessed* and saw a man who is also guilty of repeating himself. His compulsive story telling is a kind of confession, and while we don't know exactly what he did, there's an unstated war here, signaled by the early use of the phrase "before the war" (11) and later, "after the war" (31). This man is responsible for something: the fact of his birth will bring pain to others.

This is our condition.

In her essay "Portraits and Repetition," Stein says: "Is there repetition or is there insistence. I am inclined to believe there is no such thing as repetition." She explains: the fact that detective novels always have the same crime, that writers write and rewrite the same themes, that American novels have the same scenes, that books are, in fact, constantly repeating the same thing, means that "the essence of that expression is insistence, and if you insist you must each time use emphasis and if you use emphasis it is not possible while anybody is alive that they should use exactly the same emphasis."

In *Not Blessed,* the emphasis keeps shifting, word by phrase, which in turn emphasizes the text's and by extension our own, shiftiness. *Not Blessed* insists on this shift, just as it insists on sameness. Which leads us back to that strange, uncanny feeling like déjà vu, that willingness to continue despite certain meaninglessness, and that deliberate compulsion which makes us.

Teresa Carmody

Los Angeles, CA
2010

Not Blessed

Let it not be blessed.
Cursed be the man who brought tidings
To my father, saying:
'A man-child is born unto thee':
Making him very glad.

—Jeremiah 20:14-15

1

In answer to your question, I will tell you a little story: In the southern part of the country, when the space was open and when there were still people to share things with, I lived in a farmhouse with my grandmother. Often I would step outside and onto the road beside my grandmother's cottage to greet the shepherds returning with their sheep to the village. Grandmother had a fine house just outside the village, near the main road. One day I strode along the road and may have wandered off too far. I came across a policeman who did not recognize me. But I am my grandmother's grandson and I have lived in the village my whole life, I told the policeman. The question I should have asked was, who are you?

Following my question, the policeman asks if he can take me home. At this point, he believes that I am lost. The road is near my grandmother's cottage outside a village. I feel the anger and indignation swell inside me. My grandmother was one of the finest people the village had ever known.

And if this is to be a story set in contemporary times, and if this is ever to amount to anything at all, there has to be a connection with what is going on in the world today. I look at my watch and I realize that winding it is a mistake. I have to live exclusively in the past if I am to excel today—dig some fine old gems out of my suitcase.

But I may have answered irresponsibly. The policeman took me by the hand and carried me all the way back to my grandmother's cottage. I am reminded of the famous ghost story of the hunter, I believe it's a hunter, who returns home after having been missing for some significant length of time. There is a great front window that opens directly to the living room of the family house, and when the hunter finally returns home, he steps into the house through the big front window.

As an example, I wish to show you my house. It is a beautiful house, set high on a hill, and there are various reasons I live in this house. The house has faulty wiring, and yet we are able to keep lamps lit at night, in the old-fashioned manner. I remember when I first heard the saying that a house divided upon itself will fall. There are crows on the wires outside of my house, and when I was a boy I used to try and talk to them. There are other reasons I live in my house, but these reasons escape me at the moment. And if I were again given the opportunity to lecture on the subject, I would have to affirm that there are many ways of viewing things. I would have to answer the questions and be truthful and admit that all things are political, in the best sense of the word. There are, in fact, no constraints here, and there is nothing more than meaninglessness. The person with half a brain makes the best subject, I'm afraid. Am I forgetting to mention that there was a house nestled at the foot of a beautiful mountain where I spent my summers. Idyllic summers with my grandmother. My grandmother owned a lovely cottage by a lake, not far from a village. It was in this cottage that I learned most of what I still know today, what

I still believe to be true today. It was in this house, sitting by candlelight as my grandmother told me stories, that I became the person I was to become. One day, as I was taking a long and healthful walk along the road near my grandmother's cottage, a policeman suddenly appeared. The policeman, seeing a young boy alone, was immediately concerned for my well-being. The policeman took me by the hand and asked me my name and where I'd come from. I'd grown up in the village, and this exchange with the policeman came as an almost complete surprise. After all, I was one of the sons of the village, later to become a relatively prominent figure. Fascinated by these mountain paths, I spent the better part of my youth walking and reflecting on the stories my grandmother told me. It was a kind of education. The best education of all, perhaps. My grandmother's stories during the evening and then my repeating them to myself over and over again on my walks during the day.

Of course, the explanation is, thus far, insufficient. Let me explain. There were stars in the sky, or black marks. There was never enough in the way of vague answers to the more complicated questions. And when he dreamed. It was important for him to remember that physical exercise was merely a way of keeping his body fit, healthy, and trim. He'd tried to keep a written record of his dreams, a sort of dream journal, on more than one occasion. And, as a result, he had enjoyed a fair amount of notoriety up to that point in his life. It was spring and it was raining. The explanation was startling, of course. But what in the world had there ever been for people in the first place? The ground dried rapidly in the morning sun. He'd tried to keep a written record of his dreams, a sort of dream journal, on more than one occasion. Perhaps the answer was his pen. Perhaps he'd needed to purchase a better, or different, style of pen. He had been raised single-handedly by his grandmother. His grandmother lived in a mountain cottage, not far from a lake. The road outside his grandmother's cottage led to the village in one direction and to the edge of the forest in the other direction. He had lived in the village his whole life. It was summer and he would often take long and healthful walks along the road that ran past his grandmother's house. The road was very pretty. There were plants and trees and shrubs, and, depending on the time of year, a variety of wildflowers. Indeed, the road looked very pretty in the early morning mist. One day, the boy walked farther along the road than he'd ever walked before. His grandmother had forbidden him to enter the forest alone. By now, the boy could see the edge of the forest from where he stood. The boy sat on a hollowed-out log on the roadside and rested. He buried his face in his hands. Suddenly a policeman emerged from the forest. The policeman approached the boy. The policeman asked the boy if he was lost. The policeman asked the boy his name and where he'd come from. At first the boy was relieved, and then he was angry. His grandmother was one of the finest people the village had ever known. He himself would grow up and become a relatively prominent figure. He would, in fact, give the village its first measure of notoriety. How could the policeman not know who he would grow up to become.

It was early morning. There had been a serious misunderstanding. It had quickly become apparent that there was more substance to the discussions than he'd first been led to believe. He left the conference room and returned to his office extremely upset. It was spring and it was raining. It was a lot like having an angel on one's shoulder. He remembered the rule. The rule about rules. He remembered that the rules need not necessarily apply. He was lucky that way. Like he had a guardian angel on his shoulder. It was always frantic and difficult during the in-between times. He'd tried to strike a healthy balance. And quality of life was important to him. The war, it was true, had, in a manner of speaking, benefited him on a personal level. For instance, when was the last time he'd felt more awake. It was spring and it was raining. The rain fell down in sheets. Still, he attributed much of his success to a demanding and well-planned exercise regimen. It was in the time before the war. The roses bloomed in the spring rain. His home had a rustic feel, was pleasing in a rustic way, and there was war later and there was destruction later, but the memory of those early days would be what sustained him through all of his trials. His grandmother told him stories, stories he would never forget. An inquisitive boy, he would explore the fields, paths, and ponds that surrounded his grandmother's cottage. His grandmother owned a beautiful house set against forest and lake, not far from the village where he grew up. He often explored the path that led from his grandmother's house in one direction to the edge of the forest in the other direction. He often took long and healthful walks through the beautiful rolling hills that surrounded the village. One day he walked very far, farther than he'd ever walked before. He could see the edge of the forest from where he stood. His grandmother had forbidden him to enter the forest alone. Stopping to rest on a hollowed-out log that sat near the side of the road, he noticed, off in the distance, another road that he'd somehow never noticed before. The other road appeared to run parallel to the road he was on. Then he noticed a boy standing on the parallel road. The boy seemed to be around his age. Maybe a potential playmate had moved to the neighborhood. He had never had a playmate before. Maybe he would have a new friend. He had never had a friend before. Encouraged, he waved to the boy on the parallel road. Encouragingly, the boy on the parallel road waved back. Just then, a policeman emerged from the forest. Suddenly, a policeman emerged from the forest and stepped onto the road and approached the boy. The policeman approached the boy. The policeman approached the boy and asked him his name and where he'd come from. The boy told the policeman that he was from the village and that he lived in his grandmother's cottage. The policeman had never heard of his grandmother before. At first the boy was afraid, and then he was angry. How could the policeman not know who he was. His grandmother was a prominent person in the village, and he himself would eventually grow up and bring the village its first measure of notoriety.

5

For the freedom of all people. For the freedom of all people. And if he'd shouted any louder, there actually might have been someone who'd understood what the phrase meant. But people work hard. People work hard, and yet he'd done relatively well with his life. The platform was small compared to other ones he'd worked from, but that was the nature of the business: go where the people are. And in his hotel room the day before he had summoned a genie out of a bottle and asked it to grant him a wish. For all the days and all the nights that I stay alive, he asked the genie, let my body be young and healthy and handsome, and let my mind stay sharp and focused and at its peak. The genie laughed and cursed him instead. But that night he followed his exercise regimen as usual. He did sit-ups and push-ups until it was late and he was very tired. The rain on the roof woke him. The way the rain sometimes fell against the roof in complex patterns. And it was sometimes too much to bear. And sometimes people are very impolite and just don't know how to talk to others. He liked to exercise whenever possible. And when it was raining. And when the rain fell against the roof—sometimes in very complex patterns.

I wonder if I should stop and draw a picture instead, he thought to himself. He was raised by his grandmother in a house outside a small village. The cottage was not far from a lake, not far from a forest, not far from a meadow and field. One day, while taking a healthful walk along a quiet path in the meadow, he noticed another path for the very first time. The other road appeared to run parallel to the road he was on. How was it that he had not noticed the parallel road before? The boy wanted badly to cross over to the parallel road and explore. However, the parallel road seemed completely inaccessible from where he stood. Indeed, at no point did it appear that he could successfully cross over. Suddenly, another boy who seemed to be around his age appeared on the parallel road. He'd never had a playmate before and the presence of the other little boy frightened him. This day was so different from all the other days in his life and it frightened him. The boy started to run. He ran and ran. The presence of the other little boy frightened him. The boy ran and ran, farther and farther, farther along the path than he'd ever gone before. Suddenly a policeman emerged from the forest. The policeman, seeing a boy alone and so very close to the forest, tried to comfort him. The policeman gathered the boy in his arms and tried to calm the boy in a friendly voice. The policemen asked the boy his name and where he'd come from. The boy, who had at first been relieved by the policeman's sudden appearance, became more and more angry. How could this policeman not know his name. He had grown up in and around the village, and would, in fact, become a relatively famous figure, yet here was a policeman who treated him as if he were a complete unknown.

Another line of questions that hint, or prod, perhaps, a bit too strongly. It was disappointing. It was effective. It made no difference in the end. A dog chases a cat. A cat chases a mouse. Mouths chasing mouths, and so on. But the will to power, after all. And exercise. The red in his face when he'd first started following his exercise regimen in earnest. He couldn't hear a word being said. Disappointing. And bad when words are viral. And bad, really bad, when one is suffering from a broken heart. But there were other slogans that were still useful. And he could have picked another if he'd liked. Who do you speak to? Where is your mess? Do you buckle? Do you fade? You will fall apart at the very first hint of trouble. He'd heard very many negative things said about him during his life. And people do change. It was spring, and it was raining. Like a powerful potion, or serum, or any other potential cure, the days were long. The spring rain was, somehow, encouraging. It was good and healthful, he believed, to walk outside in the damp air. Yet, somehow, things had taken a turn without his quite having noticed. The way things turn sometimes. The air was wet and rainy, but good and clean, and, he believed, healthful. It was in the time before the war. As a boy he would take idyllic walks along the very lush and pretty path that ran outside his grandmother's cottage. His grandmother's house was near a large and economically significant village. He'd lived in the village his whole life. Dancing, almost, up and down the path that lead to the village, that led to the meadow, that led to the pond, it was a childhood full of good and happy memories. One day he'd set off by himself. It was a bright and cheerful morning. He thought about the ghost story his grandmother had told him the night before. The story of a hunter who'd returned home after having been missing for some significant length of time. The hunter had been away from home for so long that his family all thought that he was dead. And when the hunter returned home, he entered the house, with a giant step, through a big front window that opened directly onto the living room. The boy walked down the path toward the pond. He turned and suddenly noticed another path off in the distance that appeared to run parallel to the path he was on. He was surprised that he'd never noticed this parallel road before. The boy sat on a hollowed out log and buried his face in his hands. Then he heard leaves crack, and heavy footsteps. A boy who looked to be around his age was standing directly across from him on the parallel road. He waved at the boy, and the boy waved back. Then the boy on the parallel path ran away. He followed the boy on the parallel path as best he could. He ran and ran, but he could not catch up to the other boy. He came to the edge of the forest. His grandmother had forbidden him to enter the forest alone. A policeman stood in the middle of the road near the edge of the forest. The policeman approached the boy. He stopped in front of him. The policeman asked the boy his name and where he'd come from. The boy answered the policeman's questions politely. However, it was apparent from the beginning that the policeman thought the boy to be, at best, a lost stranger. It was outrageous. How could the policeman not know who he was. How could he have never heard of his grandmother. His grandmother had lived in the village her whole life. She was a prominent citizen and well known in and around that part of the country.

However one wishes to size it up. And there are forces in the world. He was angling for a very big promotion at the time. The spring rain was pleasant. But the line about the sand had been in the speech from the beginning. Still, he'd become increasingly belligerent, riling up the crowd, making them more and more angry. It was starting to look like a fine day after all. Indeed, there is no time like the present. And there are no visions other than the ones that are here and now. And what difference does any of it make? The loudspeaker is more important than the rain. The loudspeaker drowns out the rain. There had been talk of letting him off the hook. And that is so like you, he thought. In the present. Under present circumstances. It was decided that he was better off staying put. It was decided that he was better off remaining where he was. He thought about how nice the sky looked in the rain. His head hurt. He shut his eyes and tried to rest. He was an average looking man, though more or less handsome, he believed. He fit into crowds easily. And, in retrospect, it wouldn't have been too difficult a thing to have avoided in the first place. The loudspeaker was wet in the rain. He admitted nothing. He had developed a demanding and well thought-out exercise regimen. One that had worked well for him throughout the years. He was fit and trim and looked much younger than his years. Still, he had difficulty falling asleep. And the rain fell like tears. The ground dried rapidly from that point on. Maybe he had been too content, too satisfied, with the way things were. It was spring, and it was raining. There was the sound of rain on the roof. He found it even more difficult to sleep as the night wore on. He closed his eyes. The spring rain sounded beautiful, falling, as it did, in complex patterns against the roof. And then there was the moon, and the trees, and berries and nuts in bushes, and apples on low lying branches. He'd grown up in a small mountain village. His grandmother had raised him single-handedly in a quaint and remote cottage nestled near a road that led to a village, that led to a mountain lake, that, ultimately, led to a vast and uncharted forest. As a boy he spent most of his time taking long, solitary, and healthful walks along an idyllic country road. One day, he followed the road to a lake nestled high in the mountains. He came to the very edge of the forest. His grandmother had forbidden him to enter the forest alone. It was a cloudy day and he had walked a little farther along the road than usual. He could see the edge of the forest ahead of him, and he wondered whether or not he should turn back. Just then he heard the sound of leaves cracking, and heavy footsteps. Suddenly, he noticed another road off in the distance. The road, which the boy had never noticed before, appeared to run parallel to the road he was on. Another boy, who appeared to be about his age, was standing on the parallel road. Encouraged, he waved to the boy. Encouragingly, the boy waved back. Then the boy on the parallel road ran away. He ran and ran after the boy on the parallel road. Encouragingly, the boy waved back. He had never had a playmate before. He had never had a friend. He was almost to the edge of the forest when suddenly he saw a policeman standing in the middle of the road. The policeman gathered the boy in his arms. The policeman spoke gently to the boy. He asked the boy his name and where he'd come from. At first, the boy was very angry that the policeman pretended not to know who he was. His grandmother had lived in the village her whole life. The boy would grow up to become a famous and well-respected figure. The policeman gathered the boy in his arms. He spoke to him quite gently.

The life of the man in question has no beginning
and no end. There is movement and there is
static. There are oppositions everywhere. Late
at night he would sit at his desk and assemble
the various documents he would need for the
next day. There were documents of all kinds to
be sorted through: business letters and personal
letters, speeches, articles, scientific position
papers, academic treatises, advertisements,
greeting cards, and on and on it went. It wasn't
that the work wasn't enjoyable, it was, but the
hours he was forced to keep disrupted his exercise
schedule. He liked to sit at his work table with
his back to the open window. He liked to feel
the cool air on his neck and listen to the sounds
from the street below. But when the sounds
stopped, quieted to the point that he noticed
the silence, he would realize that it was very late
at night. On more than one occasion he was
certain that someone was watching him through
the window. When he felt this way, a cold chill
would run through his body. But he'd made it a
rule to never turn around and look. His house
was rather noisy most of the time. The cat was
exploring the bookshelves again. And the work
continued. He could honestly say that after

many years of struggling against incredible odds his powers had not lessened in any significant way. He had struggled and sacrificed mightily, but, still, yet, somehow, had persevered. He had always been a serious and inquisitive sort of boy. His grandmother had certainly thought so. A boy perhaps too serious for his own good. His grandmother. He considered himself extremely lucky. He had been raised single-handedly by his grandmother. His grandmother owned a modest cottage near the main road that led to the village in one direction and to a clear and beautiful stream in the other direction. He walked along a mountain road and skipped stones in the dirt. When he was a boy, he spent his time outdoors, happily exploring the large and small rocks, the plants and insects, and just about everything else, that existed on the road that led to the edge of the forest. Then, one day, while he was walking along the road that led to his grandmother's cottage in one direction and to the edge of the forest in the other direction, he noticed another road that seemed to run parallel to the road he was on. He thought how strange it was that he should not have noticed the parallel road before. There didn't seem to be a way to reach the parallel road from where he stood, but he could clearly see that it, like the road he was on, stretched to the edge of the forest. He decided then that he would try and find a way onto the parallel road. The boy walked much farther that day, farther than he usually walked. In fact, farther than he'd ever walked before. The boy sat on a hollowed-out log by the roadside and buried his face in his hands. Then he heard leaves crack, and heavy footsteps. A man in hunting attire approached the boy from the opposite end of the path. The man, who appeared to be a hunter, stopped directly in front of the boy and asked if he needed help. The policeman asked the boy his name and where he'd come from. He asked him if he needed help. The man said he was a policeman from the village and that it was his job to help people whenever he could. The boy began to cry. The policeman didn't know him, had never heard of his grandmother's cottage, had never even heard her name.

9

Yes, I have often been guilty of fixating too intently on people, on personality, despite how many times they have let me down. And people in general. I have observed them enough to know. There is a fire that burns inside of us, burns inside each and every one of us. Early on, I was, I admit, insecure, more insecure than I am today, obviously. I was never certain how people would react to me, to my work, to the way I looked. I was a success, yes, but, inside, I had my doubts. I eventually came to a realization though. I finally realized that the people I needed to be there for me, would indeed be there for me. After I realized this, I continued to be fascinated with people but only in the most superficial way. It is better to walk than run, I have been told. And most of the time things are far better than they appear to be. I also smoke too much. To be frank, I could have used my time more wisely. I could have taken greater pains. Still, an increasing part of me continued to strive towards being better. Towards being something bigger than myself. I decided I would try and exercise on a regular basis. It was a spring and it was raining. The spring rain was very pleasant, in its way. My grandmother had raised me single-handedly. I'd been raised by my grandmother in a small cottage near a road that led to a village in one direction and to a mountain stream in the other direction. There were only one or two other farms in that part of the country. I can still see myself as a boy, taking long and healthful walks along the road on warm summer days. At night my grandmother would tell me stories, and in the daytime I would wander along the road and repeat her stories to myself, over and over again. One day, as I was walking along the road, I noticed, for the first time, another road off in the distance that seemed to run parallel to the road I was on. I remember thinking it strange that I had never noticed this parallel road before. Although there didn't appear to be any way to reach the parallel road, I decided to try and find a way to cross over. That day I walked much farther than I had ever walked before. I followed the road to the edge of the forest, and then I stopped. My grandmother had forbidden me to enter the forest alone. I could see the neighboring farm in the distance. I remember sitting down on a large rock, a sort of boulder, and burying my face in my hands. Then I heard leaves crack, and heavy footsteps. And when I looked up, I saw a policeman standing over me. The policeman asked me my name and where I'd come from. I stood up and shook my fist at the policeman. I was very angry that the policeman did not recognize me. In fact, I had spent my entire life in and around the village. In fact, my grandmother, before her death, had been well-known in the village and all around that part of the country.

If his hair could have been styled any more appealingly, then he would certainly have had it done that way. But, still, the old doctrines were demanding. And the worries too. The worries were demanding. And the admonishments. The admonishments were worrisome and demanding. And then there were the portents. For instance, a storm was coming. People would have to run for cover. But he loved to exercise for health and fitness. Or for the greater good. And he considered himself to be an extraordinarily lucky man. In fact, it was often said that there was an angel sitting on his shoulder. His exercise regimen was good and healthy, and helped to keep him fit and trim. It was spring and it was raining. And there were worries, and there were flags and banners and trees all along the boulevards. The smallest amount of dye, though, might have sent a very powerful message. Or roguish words. The words of a rogue. A rougish look, perhaps. But in a good way. Or, better yet, a new coat and hat. Still, as it was, every word had a particular taste, had a particular value. Or, to be clear, how one hangs his coat. Or the way one wears his hat. Or how one looks at things. It was spring and it was raining. The air was very wet and cold and damp. The trucks would soon be moving out of the city. His camping chair, the flags and banners, the loudspeakers, and everything else, would soon be on their way out of the city. And what a difficult thing it was for him to end his day in such a state of mind. To end the day in such a state of mind, with such melancholic thoughts. He had always been meant for good things. The spring rain smelled fine. And he was having his hair cut, dyed, and styled. It was, in fact, a brand new day. And they'd approached him with questions about the weather. It was all so good and clear. The water. The rain. In the back of the car. Or in his office. Or at a meeting. But those were the types of things that happened to good people once in a while. The air felt especially clean that morning. He woke up feeling wonderful. There was something on the ground. He bent down and picked it up. He had been raised single-handedly by his grandmother. He had been raised by his grandmother in a beautiful house near a road that led to a mountain village in one direction and to the edge of the forest in the other direction. As a child he had spent many idyllic days exploring the road that ran near his grandmother's cottage. One day, as he was taking a healthful walk along the road, he noticed, for the very first time, another road that seemed to run parallel to the road he was on. However, there did not appear to be any way for him to reach the parallel road. Suddenly, a boy, who seemed to be about his age, appeared on the parallel road. One day another boy, who seemed to be about his age, appeared on the parallel road. But try as he might, he could not reach the other boy. He'd thought, at first, that this other boy could potentially be a new playmate or friend. He had never had a playmate before. He had never had a friend before. The boy walked along a road that led to his grandmother's cottage in one direction and to the edge of the forest in the other direction. That day he walked farther down the road than he'd ever walked before. The boy sat on a hollowed-out log by the roadside and buried his face in his hands. Then he heard leaves cracking, and heavy footsteps. The boy looked up. A policeman emerged from the forest and gathered the boy in his arms. The policeman asked the boy his name and where he'd come from. The policeman asked the boy his name. At first the boy was relieved, and then he was angry. The boy was certain that everyone in the village had heard of his grandmother. After all, she had been a very prominent person. In fact, she had lived in a cottage by the side of the road her whole life.

11

It was a time after the war. And people are more or less unkind, he thought. He was afraid of not returning home in time for supper. He'd made a complete fool of himself over the soup. There were bankers in the room, and industrialists. Other dignitaries and VIPs were present as well. It was spring and it was raining. The rain fell gently to the ground. Birds sang from the highest branches. There were birds in the trees and the spring rain fell gently to the ground. He exercised to keep himself fit and trim and looking well. His exercise regimen was good and healthy and helped to keep him fit and trim and looking well. However, there was smoke in the air. They are just blowing smoke, after all. There is no fire. And that's the problem with a broken heart, he thought. The wind blew the rain against the glass. The train, picking up steam, moved slowly out of the station. And no one will ever know exactly what tomorrow may bring. And the next day, too. And that's the problem with a broken heart, he thought. He had been raised by his grandmother in a beautiful house set high in the mountains, set near a forest, set by a lake, set just outside an economically significant village. His grandmother's house sat near a road that led to the village in one direction and to the edge of the forest in the other direction. His grandmother had forbidden him to enter the forest alone. As a boy, he would take long and healthful walks along the road that ran outside his grandmother's house. He loved to walk and explore the wilderness, all the wild areas that were near his grandmother's cottage. He would repeat his grandmother's stories to the rocks and sticks that served as his companions during the long summer months. The boy would often think of the important stories his grandmother told him, stories he would never forget. One day while the boy was taking a walk along the road that led to his grandmother's cottage in one direction and to the edge of the forest in the other direction, he noticed another road much like the road he was on. In fact, this other road seemed to run parallel to the road he was on. He couldn't understand why he hadn't noticed the parallel road before. Suddenly, another boy, who seemed to be around his age, appeared on the parallel road. The boy on the parallel road waved to him, and then, as suddenly as he'd appeared, turned and ran away. The boy ran after him, but he could not find a way to cross over to the parallel road. Suddenly, a policeman stepped out of the forest and asked the boy his name and where he'd come from. The boy stopped running, grateful, at first, for the policeman's assistance. The policeman took a giant step toward the boy. The boy started to cry. How could the policeman not have recognized him. How could he not have known his grandmother, a fine and well-respected woman who had grown very old and who had lived in the village her whole life. At first the boy was grateful for the policeman's attention, and then he was angry. He vowed that he would never let himself be humiliated in that way again. How could the policeman not have recognized him when he was destined to grow up and bring the village its first measure of notoriety.

12

He rode in the back of the car, all the while, with a brand new sense of himself. Or he was pushed. Or the problem was that he, perhaps, pushed himself too hard. At the mere mention of the police. The coffee was the first thing to go, and then the cigarettes. But he had a tremendous ability to adapt, and he knew that after the first few days back. Look, he thought, as good as new. From the back of the car. And he felt enormous satisfaction at seeing the docks and other structures that simply had not existed only a few short years before. Indeed, that part of the country had blossomed, relatively speaking, in very significant ways. He sat in his hotel room and looked at the many lights reflected on the water of the harbor below. He closed his eyes and listened to the sound of the spring rain. His room had turned out to be very adequate indeed. He was pleased. His grandmother had raised him single-handedly. He and his grandmother lived in a beautiful house just outside a small but quaint rural village. His grandmother's cottage was near the main road that led to the village in one direction and to the forest in the other direction. He had spent many idyllic childhood days exploring the fascinating natural areas that could be found along the road. Still, despite every warning, the boy followed the road almost to the edge of the lake. He had never been to the lake by himself before. His grandmother had forbidden him to enter the forest alone. There were trees and bushes and flowers and many other varieties of plants that grew along the side of the road. He wanted to talk to the boy on the parallel road. He thought that he might have found a potential playmate. He had never had a playmate before. He had never had a friend before. He waved, but the boy on the parallel road did not wave back. Soon he heard leaves cracking, and heavy footsteps. He looked up and saw a policeman coming toward him from the opposite end of the road. The policeman had been hunting in the forest and had his kill slung over his shoulder in the manner of a sack. The policeman approached the boy and asked him his name and where he'd come from. At first the boy was relieved, and then he was angry. His grandmother had been a prominent member of the village. He had lived in the village his whole life. How could the policeman not know who he would become. How could the policeman, at the very least, not have recognized his grandmother's name.

13

And it is high time I made myself more clear. Forgive me for having been, thus far, obscure. In fact, I did not mean to lie. In fact, I meant to do the opposite. I mean always to tell the truth. It's just that your line of questioning has been excellent and has allowed me an opportunity to reflect on the past, to remember that there are many different ways of viewing the past. Indeed, I have come to realize, yet again, that certain principles need constant restating in order to be understood. For instance, in violation of the law. Or how certain acts of indecency were, at first, construed. Hence, the page turns. The story continues. If even only in outline. Why, the mere mention of it causes me to shudder. But if one carefully studies the footnotes. And every word was an act, or rather, a movement towards persuasion. Rather put together, don't you think? But let me put it to you still more clearly. There is a version of events that will haunt us even in our darkest hours. Even in our wildest dreams. Hence, the page turns. And the story continues. If even only in outline. And I am afraid, however, that everything must change. Change is for the better. I am afraid. But that is not how I would characterize my life and work. My struggles having long been overcome. But still I would characterize my life somewhat differently. I would start, of course, with my grandmother. A strong and wise woman. She was my single greatest influence. I was raised by her single-handedly. She was a prominent member of the village where I grew up. She had a beautiful house near the road that led to the village where I grew up in one direction and to the edge of the forest in the other direction. My grandmother used to tell me stories. Her stories were filled with bits of wisdom that I remember, that guide me, to this very day. One day, while I was out walking on the road that led to the edge of the forest, I stopped to admire a young jay nesting in a tree. While I stood on my tippy-toes, straining to make out the jay's nest on a branch, I saw, nestled in the brush, a remote hunter's cabin that I had never noticed before. A small boy, who appeared to be about my age, stood in front of the cabin, whittling wood with a knife. The cabin sat on a road that appeared to run parallel to the one I stood on. Try as I might, I could not get the attention of the boy whittling the wood. Indeed, I could not get him to look up and take notice of me. The cabin, and thus the boy, appeared to be inaccessible from the road I was on. I then remember hearing leaves crack and heavy footsteps behind me. I turned around and saw a tall policeman. The policeman asked me my name and where I'd come from. At first I was relieved, and then I was angry. My grandmother had lived in and around the village her whole life, and I could not believe that I should be taken for a stranger by this tall policeman. Surely he must have lived to regret his mistake. The policeman would have to lie over and over again to avoid telling the true story of our meeting that day by the lake. I would, in fact, grow up and become a relatively famous man. I would, in fact, bring the village its first measure of notoriety.

14

It was one fiction after another, and it began to
bother him. It was spring and it was raining.
There was a bird nestled in a tree. He had no
choice but to talk, to continue talking. And there
is only so much, he thought, that can be done in
a single day. Indeed there is only so much that
one can hope to accomplish in a single day. Then
he began to sing. He created a list of everything
he'd ever done. Every notion that had ever
occurred to him. He talked all night. The spring
rain sounded pretty falling against the roof. And
he'd managed, even in that day and age, and even
when all seemed lost. A real world full of real
events. It seemed strange. Pretty, but making
complex patterns, nonetheless. It was spring and
the rain fell on the roof in a particularly pretty
way. I think not magic, he managed to say. But
otherwise. And however one wishes to carry on.
Why, after one makes the choice to carry on.
There is grace in knowing. And then he closed
his eyes. His grandmother had raised him single-
handedly. His grandmother had been a great
and extraordinarily wise woman. A prominent
citizen in an economically significant village.
His grandmother was the greatest single person
he had ever known. His grandmother had raised

him single-handedly in a beautiful house near the village where he'd grown up. The road led to the forest in one direction and past a great lake in the other direction. There were farms in the neighborhood, but they were well separated, and he'd had little contact with the other residents in the area throughout most of his life. One day while exploring the road that led to the edge of the forest, he remembered a story his grandmother had told him the night before. The story was about a hunter who'd been away from his family for some significant length of time. The family all believed the hunter to be dead. The family lived in a house with a great front window that opened directly on the living room. One evening at dusk, the hunter unexpectedly returned. The hunter entered the house. The hunter took a giant step and entered the house through a great front window. Suddenly, the boy saw a road that he had never seen before. This new and unexpected road appeared to run parallel to the road he was on. Yet there was no way for the boy to cross over to the parallel road. So he repeated his grandmother's story to himself and ran and ran as fast as he could. He ran and ran until he was out of breath. He sat on a rock and buried his face in his hands. Then he heard leaves cracking, and heavy footsteps. A policeman approached him from the opposite end of the road. The policeman appeared to have been hunting and carried his kill slung over his shoulder in the manner of a sack. The policeman asked the boy his name and where he'd come from. At first the boy was relieved, and then he was angry. The boy would grow up and bring the village its first measure of notoriety. His grandmother was a prominent citizen in an economically significant village. How could the policeman not see who he was destined to become. He'd lived in the village his whole life. The policeman gathered the boy in his arms. He comforted the boy and dried his tears. I will lead you in the right direction, the policeman told the boy. I will help you find your way home.

15

And now to pick up where I left off. It was a
suspicion I'd chosen to act upon. But the flood
of emotion was killing me. And, in a way, I
couldn't believe my own audacity. But the flood
of emotion was killing me. Years before, I'd had
a similar experience. I was positive then, too,
that I felt things, perhaps, too severely. I was
obviously incorrect. I think it was the work, the
pressure of the war, the entire situation at the
time. The period, of course, is well documented.
Incidentally, I am currently reviewing some of
the documents from that era for my memoir.
We were very young, and, if I may be frank, a
bit out of control. It was the times. There was
so much going on in the world. My head would
just explode at the thought. The very thought.
It was exciting. I believe that anyone would have
felt exactly the way I felt. Indeed, just the thought
of those times gives me a tingling sensation in
my neck and spine. I am reminded of a night
not long ago. It was spring and it was raining.
This was in the time before the war. I was raised
by my grandmother, raised in my grandmother's
beautiful house near the village where I grew up.
My grandmother owned a most beautiful house.
Her cottage was just off the main road that led

to the village in one direction and to the edge of the forest in the other direction. It was an idyllic life for a young man. My grandmother was full of wisdom and understanding and knowledge. She would tell me stories. These stories built my character and shaped the person I am today. There was one story in particular. It was the story of a hunter who'd left his family. The hunter had been away from his family for a significant length of time. The hunter's family was certain that he was dead. Eventually, the hunter returned to his family home, but instead of coming in through the front door like any other person would, he entered the house through an enormous front window that led directly into the living room. On still another occasion, I was walking along the road outside my grandmother's house, gathering rocks and exploring, like I often did in those days, when suddenly I noticed another road off in the distance. This other road appeared to run parallel to the road I was on. Suddenly, another boy who seemed to be about my age appeared on the parallel road. I waved to the boy, but the boy did not wave back. I waved to the boy on the parallel road, and then, just as suddenly as he'd appeared, the boy ran away. I ran and ran after the boy for as long as I could. I wanted to ask him if he'd be my new playmate. I'd never had a playmate before. I'd never had a friend. I was almost at the edge of the forest. My grandmother had forbidden me to enter the forest alone, so I stopped running and sat on a hollowed-out log and buried my face in my hands. Just then, a policeman emerged from the forest and approached me. The policeman stopped in front of me and asked me my name and where I'd come from. I was, at first, relieved to see the policeman, and then I was angry. The policeman gathered me in his arms and tried to comfort me. He assured me that he would show me the way home. I was, however, becoming increasingly angry. I was outraged by the conduct of this policeman. How could he not know who I was. I was, after all, destined to grow up and become a more or less prominent figure. My grandmother, having lived in the area her whole life, was well respected in and around the village. To this day, I do not know if the policeman understood my anger. I was so young then, at that point.

16

I did obey. For a long time I did everything I was asked to do. But there was a small problem. I was no longer free. I was being subjected to a process, a course of action, that's sole purpose, it seemed, was to torment me. Torment was, of course, my subjective characterization of the process, of what occurred. And I do admit that I was more than a little surprised. Indeed what I discovered was a surprise. But a process, in those days. A particular course of action. Still, it was hard to remember what was expected of me from one day to the next. In the back seat of the car. I was often dishonest. It was spring and it was raining. I listened to the rain fall against the windshield. It sounded pretty. And I tried my best to keep up, but it seemed to me that even my own rather excellent memory had, at that point, become somewhat unreliable. Thinking now about that particular set of circumstances. I had almost forgotten. I was very young. I was raised single-handedly by my grandmother. She owned a beautiful house near the village where I grew up. Her house was situated by the main road that led to the village in one direction and to the forest in the other direction. The incident, or the memory of it, that I'm referring to is something that happened one summer while I was staying at my grandmother's cottage near an old fishing village, not far from a great lake. My grandmother's house was near the road that led to the village in one direction and to the meadow in the other direction. Her house was not far from a large, vast, and, seemingly, to my youthful eyes, bottomless lake. One beautiful spring morning, I was out taking a long and healthful walk along the road when it began to rain. To this day, I still remember the many things my grandmother taught me. She was the wisest of women and often told me stories. I remember one day in particular. I had suddenly observed a new road, an additional road, if you will, that appeared to run parallel to the road I was on. I had never seen this parallel road before, though I had spent much of my youth exploring the area. Quite mysteriously, a young boy about my age suddenly appeared on the parallel road. He waved to me. I had no playmates, having been raised single-handedly by my grandmother. I had, in fact, never had a playmate. I had never had a friend. I waved back to the boy on the parallel road and looked for a way to cross over to speak to him. Suddenly the boy on the parallel road turned and ran away. I ran and ran after the boy, but I could not catch up to him. Try as I might, I still could not find a way to cross over to the parallel road. When I reached the edge of the forest, I stopped. My grandmother had forbidden me to enter the forest alone. I rested on a hollowed-out log that sat on the roadside. I buried my face in my hands. It was then that I was approached by a policeman who had suddenly appeared on the opposite end of the road in the direction of the forest. The policeman approached me and asked me my name and where I'd come from. Then he gathered me in his arms. At first, I felt relieved, and then I became angry. How could the policeman have failed to recognize me. My name would eventually bring the village its first measure of notoriety. My grandmother was a very prominent figure in those parts, having spent her whole life in and around the village.

17

Explosions and smoke and fire, yes. But, still, somehow, magnificently, a real leveling off of the fear factor. At least in some circles. It was spring and it was raining, pleasantly, one afternoon. He didn't talk much about himself. At least not at first. But that's the way it is with a broken heart, he thought. The spring rain fell gently to the ground. It was pleasant to be out in the rain. It was pleasant to be walking again, especially on a beautiful spring afternoon. And people eventually, inevitably, hated themselves for believing what they believed. But that's the way it is with a broken heart, he thought. There was no one left for him to impress. He sat behind the wheel for a moment and then he started the engine. The way the rain fell in the springtime. And birds were singing. He was thinking how it took a really long time to mend a broken heart. And the spring rain sounded pretty falling against the roof. The feeling of falling, too, like the rain, or the feeling of skating on thin ice. Why, the very moment you think you have it. And new positions to try. It was all very precise, or it all required a level of precision, a great deal of precision. There was a lot riding on it. A lot at stake. And you must always know what you are talking about and to whom you are talking. And precision. And attention to detail. But that's the way it is with a broken heart, he thought. And mending a broken heart is not so easy, after all, he thought. He was raised single-handedly by his grandmother. His grandmother used to tell him stories when he was a boy. He was raised by his grandmother in a beautiful house just outside the village where he grew up. He used to sit up late into the night and listen to his grandmother's stories. His grandmother's cottage was near the main road that led to the village in one direction and to a pasture in the other direction. He would take long and healthful walks along the road every summer day. Every spring day he used to take long and healthful walks along the road that led to his grandmother's cabin in one direction and to the edge of a large, vast, and, to his youthful eyes, seemingly bottomless lake in the other direction. One day, as he was walking along the road, he suddenly noticed another road off in the distance. This other road appeared to run parallel to the road he was on. There was a house on the parallel road, and a boy who seemed to be about his age was standing in front of the house. He waved at the boy, excitedly. He had never had a playmate before. He had never had a friend. Then, suddenly, the boy ran away. At first the boy was frightened, and then he was relieved. A policeman suddenly emerged from the forest and sat down beside him. The boy sat on a hollowed-out log and buried his face in his hands. The policeman gathered the boy in his arms and tried to comfort him. He asked the boy his name and where he'd come from. The boy was, at first, relieved, and then he was angry. He had no playmates. He had never had a playmate before. He had never had a friend. He was raised single-handedly by his grandmother. Still the policeman should have known who he was. He would soon grow up and become a relatively prominent figure. He would, in fact, give the village its first measure of notoriety. His grandmother had lived in the village her whole life and was well known in that part of the country. The policeman gathered the boy in his arms.

18

There was a break in the weather. It was subtle and easy to miss. But anyone who was paying attention would have recognized the change in the weather for what it was, for what it seemed to represent. It was spring and it was raining. But still a night to remember. The night before. The night after. Nights to remember in general. But who would remember. It was a way of looking at the world, though. And what was the point. He sat in the car for a moment, and then he started the engine. A system so complicated that no one could imagine actually trying to understand it. Or just plain folks. And it paid to consider the source of one's information, he thought. There was a great deal of betting at the window. At the table, a moment of fantastic competition. Competitive energy. And then things slowed down because things inevitably slow down. There was a change in the weather. A lovely spring rainstorm. And the sink in the kitchen was broken and needed to be fixed. There were crows gathered on a wire, and he used to love to try and talk to the crows, to hear what they were saying. It was spring and it was raining. A lovely and gentle sort of rain. A reminder of what was. His hat was in his hands. He was raised single-handedly by his grandmother. His grandmother owned a beautiful house just outside an economically significant village. His grandmother's cottage was near the main road that led to the village in one direction and to the edge of the forest in the other direction. He would spend his summer days exploring the road and remembering the stories his grandmother told him. His favorite was the story of the hunter. The hunter's family lived in a beautiful house with an unusually large front window. The hunter was thought dead, but he wasn't dead, and he eventually returned home. And when the hunter returned home, he entered the family's house through the great front window. The hunter entered the house through the enormous front window with one giant step. One day the boy was taking a healthful and restorative walk along the road when he suddenly noticed another road that appeared to run parallel to the road he was on. How it surprised the boy to see the parallel road. The boy followed the parallel road, but he could not find a place to cross over. His grandmother had forbidden him to enter the forest alone. He sat on a rock on the roadside and buried his face in his hands. Suddenly, a policeman emerged from the forest and approached the boy. A policeman suddenly emerged from the forest. The policeman stopped in front of the boy and asked him his name and where he'd come from. At first the boy was relieved, and then he was angry. The boy was angry when he realized that the policeman didn't know who he was. Soon the boy would grow up and become a relatively prominent figure. He would grow up to give the village its first measure of notoriety. His grandmother was a great woman and had spent her entire life in the village. It was impossible that the policeman would not know who he was. The policeman gathered the boy in his arms. The policeman gathered the boy in his arms and tried to comfort him. Soon the boy would grow up and become well-known in and around the village.

19

There was never any mention of him in the books, which was to be expected. Yet he was neither a parasite nor a nobody. From his bedroom window, he could see the road outside. He remembered the trucks with banners and the loudspeakers. He looked away. But he could still remember the sounds. This is a false start, he thought. He had to find his way back to the beginning, for the beginning was where things always started. There was an open door. Someone entered the room. There was a ceramic figure on the window sill, directly next to a small flower pot. He was at home. Still, the thought of it frightened him. He had to maintain his composure. No one remembered him. No one would remember him. The things others had done before were of no concern. He was reading a book for pleasure, a book about spies. The future and the past. And things seemed to be getting a bit confused. He had to remember which way to go. There was an open door. He hung his head. He remembered the beginning. At one time the café was open until three. He remembered something his grandmother had told him when he was a young boy. His grandmother had owned a beautiful house. He'd been raised single-handedly by his grandmother in a beautiful house. The house was close to the village. The house was near a road that led to the village in one direction and to the edge of the forest in the other direction. He'd often walk along the road and think of the stories his grandmother told him. His grandmother owned a beautiful house near a village, and one day he went outside for a walk. He walked along the road that led to the edge of the forest in one direction and to his grandmother's house in the other direction. He thought about a story his grandmother had told him. He often thought about the stories his grandmother told him. His favorite was the story of the hunter who'd disappeared. The hunter's family was certain that he was dead. One day while he was out walking on the road that led to his grandmother's house in one direction and to the edge of the forest in the other direction, he suddenly saw another road that he'd never seen before. This other road appeared to run parallel to the road he was on. The boy looked up and down the parallel road but could not see a way to cross over. He ran and ran. The boy took a walk along the road that ran outside his grandmother's cottage. He sat on a hollowed-out log and buried his face in his hands. And when he looked up, he saw a policeman approach him. The boy looked up and saw a policeman approach him. A policeman suddenly emerged from the forest and asked him his name and where he'd come from. At first the boy was relieved. The policeman gathered him up in his arms. At first the boy was relieved, and then he was angry. How could the policeman not have recognized him. He would grow up and become a prominent figure. He would grow up to give the village its first measure of notoriety. The policeman would regret his actions that day. In the future the policeman would be forced to lie to his family and friends at the tavern. He would change the story. He would have to change the story. His grandmother had been a prominent figure in the area and, what was more, had lived in the village her whole life. He himself would grow up and become a relatively prominent figure.

20

If my answers have not been exactly what you wanted, then I apologize. But it has always been my policy to be as thorough as humanly possible. To begin again, the birds do not make as much noise as they used to. There is not as much room for them in my house these days, I'm afraid, and there is no way to set the birds loose so they can fly away. And this relates directly to what I said earlier about there being many ways of viewing things. But I flatter myself. My success had more to do with personality than anything else, I fear. Still, I conducted myself politely and respectfully whenever I could. It wasn't always possible though, to be sure. I have typically been engaged in investigations that cannot be put on hold for any reason, and many times practical considerations have had to be set aside. Yet, in the end, of course, I am quite often proven correct. But, my apologies, I have digressed again. You had a very specific question. Let me see if I can answer. When the wall goes up I have to examine every single little thing that may or may not have occurred. I have to be certain, you see. Being as busy as I am, I have to be certain that I don't overlook even the smallest details. I have to be certain that what I build is real, that I have not, in fact, lied to myself by engaging what is not real, so to speak. My grandmother was a woman of great insight. I owe much of what I know to her, to her stories, to what she told me. My grandmother's house was near the village where I grew up. My grandmother thought very highly of me and would often tell me stories. My grandmother's house was close to the main road that led to the village in one direction and to a great stream in the other direction. From time to time, I would go out to explore, and sometimes I ventured farther along the road than was wise. Once I was very near the edge of the forest when, suddenly, I spotted a strange road that I had never seen before. This other road appeared to run parallel to the road I was on. I wanted to cross over to the parallel road, but I could find no access point. Suddenly, a boy who seemed to be about my age appeared on the parallel road. Encouragingly, the boy on the parallel road stood and waved to me. However, when I waved back, the boy ran away. I had never had a playmate before. I had never had a friend before. My grandmother raised me single-handedly. My grandmother's house was near a village. There was a stream and a river. There were many other farmhouses that stood nearby. I ran after the boy on the parallel road until I reached the edge of the forest. I remember sitting on a hollowed-out log and burying my face in my hands. Suddenly, a policeman emerged from the forest. I could see from his manner of dress and the kill he had slung over his shoulder, in the manner of a sack, that he had been in the forest hunting. The policeman tried to comfort me. He asked me my name and where I'd come from. Then he gathered me up in his arms. He asked me my name. I began to cry. How could the policeman not know who I was. My grandmother had spent her whole life in the village. I would eventually grow up and bring the village its first measure of notoriety. Someday, I vowed, the policeman would come to regret his actions. He would have to change his story. He would have tell his friends at the tavern who I was and what I had grown up to become. I had walked farther that day than I had ever walked before. My grandmother had forbidden me to go to the lake alone. My grandmother had forbidden me to enter the forest alone. The policeman would be punished and I would grow up and bring the village its first measure of notoriety.

21

It was no wonder things went the way they did. The radio installation, including the large array of towers, was destined to fall apart. He'd had a premonition. He'd been having strange dreams for weeks. Indeed, losing things, as it were, as if the times had changed. Perhaps it was due to a lack of direct communication. When he was younger he had been more passionate. The time before the war had, in fact, been, generally, more passionate. And nothing could stop him. His career blossomed overnight. And no one could question his passion, his commitment, not then, not at that time. How passionate he was. He'd learned to be responsible. He'd learned to work by himself. He certainly didn't have time to dwell over lost things. But he was older now. There was treasure hidden in the garden, if only one cared to look. He kept to himself. The radio broadcasts would continue for some time, or so it seemed. He found himself spending more and more time improving his appearance, exercising to keep fit and trim. He had had a magical childhood. Even when there wasn't money for anything else. His grandmother lived in a house near a lake. An elaborate cottage and farmyard complex. His grandmother's beautiful house.

Her wise stories. His grandmother owned a beautiful house outside the village where he grew up. The village would later play a small but significant role in the overall economic development of the area. He had lived in the village his whole life. His grandmother's house was near a road that led to the village in one direction and to the forest in the other direction. He would often take healthful walks along the road that ran outside his grandmother's house. There was a lake set deep in a forest. One day while he was walking along the road that led to the edge of the forest in one direction and to his grandmother's house in the other direction, he noticed another road that appeared to run parallel to the road he was on. He had never noticed the parallel road before. There was a small farmhouse on the parallel road. A boy who appeared to be about his age stood in front of the farmhouse. The boy waved to him in a friendly way, but when he waved back, the boy ran away. He ran and ran after the boy on the parallel road. He ran and ran until he reached the edge of the lake. His grandmother had forbidden him to enter the forest alone. He sat on a hollowed-out log by the edge of the forest and buried his face in his hands. The boy began to cry. Suddenly, he looked up and saw a policeman approach him from the opposite end of the road. The policeman stopped in front of him and asked him his name and where he'd come from. The policeman gathered the boy in his arms. At first the boy was relieved, and then he was angry. How could the policeman not have recognized him. His grandmother was well-known in that part of the country. She'd lived in the village her whole life. He had never had a playmate before. He had never had a friend. He used to repeat his grandmother's stories to the rocks and sticks that kept him company when he went outside to play. The policeman gathered the boy in his arms. The policeman slung the boy over his shoulder, in the manner of a sack, and carried him home. At first the boy was relieved, and then he was angry.

22

And that's the way it is with a broken heart, he thought. He laughed. He laughed and laughed. He laughed himself good and silly. But that's the way it is with a broken heart, he thought. Still, there is nothing in it for people. Is there? There is nothing good there for people. Is there? And he had his hat in his hands. And he was lying under the trees. A canopy of branches. The way he tied his tie. Or how he often looked at himself in the mirror. It was spring and it was raining. Pursing his lips. The spring rain fell in complex patterns against the roof. His exercise regimen was good and healthful and had helped to keep him fit and trim and looking much younger than his years. It was spring and it was raining. How many years had it been since he'd first come to see things that way? Still, the way he always wore his heart on his sleeve got him all kinds of special notice. He had his hat in his hands. He pulled his collar up against the rain. He looked himself up and down in the mirror. He pursed his lips. And when you are talking to someone for the very first time. The way they make you think bad things about yourself. It's like being scolded, or, rather, protected against the part of yourself that you value most. Boiled, even, in a way. And when you are talking to someone else for the very first time. But, then, that's the way it is with a broken heart. The region was, more or less, famous for its large variety of fruit-bearing trees. There were nuts and berries slung on low branches as far as the eye could see. And if only I could control the weather, he thought to himself with a laugh. Fundamentally, it was just good to be out and around people again, he thought. His grandmother owned a beautiful house near an economically significant village. His grandmother had lived in the village her whole life. He had been raised single-handedly by his grandmother. His grandmother owned a small but beautiful cottage that was nestled at the foot of a mountain, not far from the village where he grew up. The village was very small but more or less important. The village had played a significant role in the economic development of the entire area. His grandmother's house was near a road that led to the village in one direction and to the forest in the other direction. The policeman gathered the boy in his arms. As a boy, he would take long and healthful walks along the road that led to his grandmother's house in one direction and to a vast and, to his youthful eyes, seemingly endless orchard of fruit trees in the other direction. He often walked along the road and thought about the stories his grandmother told him. One fine spring day he was walking along the road when, for the first time, he noticed another road that appeared to run parallel to the road he was on. The door to the farmhouse opened and a boy who seemed to be about his age stepped outside. Encouraged, he waved to the boy, but the boy did not wave back. He had never had a playmate before. He had never had a friend before. Suddenly, the boy on the parallel road ran away. The boy sat down on a hollowed-out log and buried his face in his hands. Then he heard leaves crack, and heavy footsteps. And when he looked up he saw a policeman approach him from the opposite end of the road. The policeman sat down beside him and asked him his name and where he'd come from. At first the boy was relieved, and then he was angry. The policeman gathered the boy in his arms. The village had played a small but significant role in the economic development of the entire area. How could the policeman not have recognized him. His grandmother had lived in the village her whole life. His grandmother often told him stories that he would never forget.

23

To thrive during such times demands a certain kind of temperament, a certain type of intellect and, of course, a certain amount of good fortune. The system had been in place for almost a generation. And the tendencies and limitations inherent in the system's operation had certainly been identified, yet attempts to refine the system, to make it run more smoothly, had consistently been met with failure. The most critical limitation of the system identified to date was its dependency, despite the concept of dependency itself being a fundamental component of the system's design. He put his pen down. The rest would have to wait. For now he was content to let his mind wander. There were a lot of things he had to do when he got home. It was spring and it was raining. The driver picked him up every morning right before dawn. It was spring and it was raining. It was dangerous on the road. There was never enough money to buy new things. He took a long walk in the spring rain. His grandmother had owned a beautiful house near the village where he'd grown up. He had been raised single-handedly by his grandmother. He'd lived in the village his whole life. His grandmother often told him stories. His grandmother's cottage was near a road that led to the village in one direction and to the forest in the other direction. As a boy, he would take long and healthful walks along the road that ran just outside his grandmother's large kitchen window. As a boy, he'd spend hours and hours exploring the road. He would take healthful walks to the lake, to the river, to the forest. His grandmother had forbidden him to enter the forest alone. His grandmother often told him stories. One day while he was walking along the road, exploring, he saw another road that he had never seen before. This new road appeared to run parallel to the road he was on. The boy ran and ran. The road led to his grandmother's house in one direction and to a vast and, to his youthful eyes, seemingly endless orchard of fruit trees in the other direction. He sat on a hollowed-out log and buried his face in his hands. Suddenly, a policeman approached him from the opposite end of the road. The policeman, in the manner of a hunter, had fresh game slung over his shoulder. The policeman gathered the boy in his arms. His grandmother had lived in the village her whole life. It was impossible to understand how the policeman could not have recognized him. He would grow up to give the village its first measure of notoriety. He would bring the village its first measure of notoriety. The policeman asked him his name and where he'd come from. The policeman gathered the boy in his arms. At first the boy was relieved, and then he was angry. At first the boy was relieved, and then he was angry. He'd lived in the village his whole life. How could the policeman have failed to recognize him.

24

Because it was an island, or because it was a country, or because it was a small country, or because there were so many dignitaries gathered in the room at the time. His commentary was cold. Thus each account was easily recognizable, even if one had, in fact, never actually seen the place before. There was much rushing about then, much hustling towards something as yet not identified. Things were, however, powerful and new, no one could deny that. The way in which, for instance, a door opened and closed. Or informing people. But, then, there really was nothing in it for people. Was there? But then, informing people was something in and of itself, after all. A thing all by itself. A principle in and of itself. Like eating bacon and eggs. Like always having to eat certain kinds of food for breakfast. It was spring and it was raining. It was pleasant to be standing in the rain. The smell of the rain in the springtime was extraordinary. There were very many people gathered outside. But then, there really was nothing in it for people. Was there? It was spring and it was raining. Or it was pleasant in the garden. He couldn't remember which way he had come, how he'd ever got to that point. He'd been raised single-handedly by his grandmother. His grandmother owned a beautiful house near the village where he grew up. The house was near a road that led to the village in one direction and to the forest in the other direction. The boy would often wander along the road and remember the stories his grandmother had told him. One day, he was wandering along the road thinking about the stories his grandmother had told him when he suddenly saw a road he had never seen before. This new road appeared to run parallel to the road he was on. The boy looked and looked but he could not find a way to cross over to the parallel road. The boy followed the parallel road to the edge of the forest. His grandmother had forbidden him to enter the forest alone. The boy sat on a large rock and buried his face in his hands. Suddenly, a policeman emerged from the forest with freshly killed game slung over his shoulder, in the manner of a sack. The policeman approached the boy from the opposite end of the road. At first the boy was relieved, and then he was angry. The policeman asked the boy his name and where he'd come from. At first the boy was relieved, and then he was angry. The policeman gathered the boy in his arms. At first the boy was relieved, and then he was angry. How could the policeman not have recognized him. He would grow up to give the village its first measure of notoriety. His grandmother had lived in the village her whole life. The policeman would eventually pay for what he'd done. He would have to lie to his friends at the tavern, he would have to lie to his family. One day the policeman would have to change his story. He would have to lie about what had happened that day in the forest.

25

And the question quickly came to haunt him. The color of his umbrella against the sky. Or, its outline, so to speak. Or even a potion, or a serum, or some other kind of cure. In fact, a fixation on creating something perfect. A perfect day. The memory of which was just out of reach. It was spring and it was raining. The mockingbird sang. A beautiful day, nonetheless. There was an electricity in the air that reminded him of the time before the war. Flags and banners. The platform. Trucks in the streets with loudspeakers. He had managed to get everything he'd wanted then. And there was a buzz in the air. One question remained, however. And things were very different from that point on. There was, in fact, some difference he couldn't quite put his finger on. Certainly there was sufficient noise, but for some reason the noise was distracting. The noise was making it difficult for him to concentrate. And one could put the pieces of the puzzle together, make them fit, just as easily. Something like a mosaic. It was sad. Though, of course, he would never find out why. The answer would simply never occur to him. Taking a coin out of his pocket. A thin coin. And he had to gather himself quickly. Flip the coin high in the air. His grandmother had raised him single-handedly. His grandmother owned a beautiful house near an economically significant village. He was raised by his grandmother. His grandmother's cottage was near a road that led to the village in one direction and to the forest in the other direction. He would sit by the lake for hours and think about the stories his grandmother had told him. He spent many healthful hours wandering up and down the road. The road that ran outside his grandmother's cottage had many interesting sights and features. Then one day as he was wandering along the road he saw another road off in the distance that he had never seen before. This new road appeared to run parallel to the road he was on. However, there did not appear to be any way for him to cross over to the parallel road. He ran and ran and tried to keep up with the boy on the parallel road. He had never had a playmate before. He had never had a friend. When he reached the edge of the forest, the boy stopped. His grandmother had forbidden him to enter the forest alone. He sat on a hollowed-out log and buried his face in his hands. Then he heard leaves crack, and heavy footsteps. A policeman approached the boy from the opposite end of the road. The policeman stopped in front of the boy and asked him his name and where he'd come from. At first the boy was relieved. The policeman gathered the boy in his arms. Then the boy became angry. How could the policeman not recognize him. He would grow up to become a relatively prominent figure and provide the village with its first measure of notoriety. His grandmother had spent her whole life in the village. The boy started to say something and then stopped himself. The boy began to cry. At first the boy was relieved, and then he began to cry.

26

A particularly rainy spring day, yes. But, then, the rain always fell more powerfully in the spring. It was spring and it was raining. I remember it well. I used to dress very nicely when it rained. I would go outside. And appearances were very important in those days. In fact, I looked forward to rainy days for just that reason. I would stand in the rain and think about people I'd met in passing. The hustle and bustle. And there were, in fact, many intriguing people, passers-by and the like, on the streets, in those days. I would stand in the rain, and sometimes in the wind, and consider the people who were interesting to me. Before the radio became popular. Before the proliferation of the loudspeaker. Even as a boy I enjoyed standing in the rain. I didn't have a car. I enjoyed standing in the rain even when I was a boy. I had no playmates, no real friends, but I would make up stories and tell my stories to the rocks and sticks that I found on the ground. I listened to the crows talk to one another on the trees, on the wires, and I tried to talk back to them in a crow's voice. But I was a boy, so I couldn't really talk to crows at all. Before the radio was widely available. I exercised often to keep myself fit, trim, and in good health. My grandmother owned a beautiful house. We used to tell each other stories. My grandmother told me stories I would never forget. I still remember my grandmother's stories. Her cottage was near the main road that led to the village in one direction and to the edge of the forest in the other direction. I would often wander on the road and pretend that my grandmother's stories were my own stories. I would play with rocks and sticks and pretend to talk to the crows. I had no other playmates then. No friends to speak of. Then one day, while I was walking along the road, a most extraordinary thing happened. I looked off into the distance and suddenly saw a road I had never seen before. The road appeared to run parallel to the road I was on. I continued my walk, all the while keeping an eye upon the parallel road. I looked and looked, but there did not appear to be a way to cross over to the parallel road. Then I saw a red farmhouse on the parallel road. A boy who appeared to be about my age stepped out the front door of the farmhouse and, encouragingly, waved at me. Encouraged, I waved back. But the boy ran away. I ran and ran after the boy. I ran until I reached the edge of the lake. My grandmother had forbidden me to enter the forest alone. I remember sitting on a hollowed-out log and burying my face in my hands. I was surprised when I looked up. I was surprised to see a policeman suddenly approach me. The policeman approached me from the opposite end of the road, from the direction of the forest. He stopped in front of me and asked me my name and where I'd come from.

At first I was relieved, and then I was angry. The policeman gathered me up in his arms and tried to comfort me. At first I was relieved, and then I was angry. It was an outrage to think that the policeman didn't know who I was. I was to become a relatively prominent figure. My grandmother was well-respected in and around the lake district. In fact, my grandmother had lived in the village her whole life. I wanted to punish the policeman for his indiscretion, for his inability to perform his duty in a manner consistent with what I expected. At first I was relieved, and then I was angry. The policeman asked me my name. My grandmother had forbidden me to enter the forest alone. I remember I sat on a hollowed-out log and waved to the boy on the parallel road, and then I buried my face in my hands and began to cry.

27

Eventually every mystery is solved. But without narration. And without a specific voice to guide the reader. However, without noise, without air and sound, there is no one left. No one. Eventually he was able to repeat everything he knew. And every irrelevancy was recorded. And the point was that between irrelevancies various truths could be discovered. The mystery would be solved. He had to get back to his house at some point. He was always the type to think of the perfect retort too late, in the car on the way home, for instance. And, as was his style, he turned one thing into another. One thought into another. The driver would ask him a question and he would answer. Exercise kept him healthy, trim, and fit. The driver would ask him a question. He'd told the story many times before. He told the story whenever he was asked questions he didn't care to answer. It was the story of a hunter. It was spring and it was raining. The rain was nice and made the day pleasant. His grandmother owned a beautiful farmhouse. His grandmother's cottage was near an important and economically significant fishing village. He'd been raised single-handedly by his grandmother. His grandmother had raised him in a beautiful cottage not far from the village where he'd grown up. His grandmother's house was next to a road that led to the village in one direction and to the edge of the forest in the other direction. He often took long and healthful walks along the road. One day as he was wandering along the road, he began to remember the stories his grandmother had told him. One story concerned a hunter. The boy wandered along the road that led to the village in one direction and to a vast and, to his youthful eyes, seemingly endless orchard of fruit trees in the other direction. The boy looked up and suddenly saw another road that appeared to run parallel to the road he was on. He had grown up in and around the village. The boy looked up and saw a policeman approach him from the opposite end of the road. The policeman gathered the boy in his arms. He could no longer see the boy on the parallel road. And he began to cry. The policeman asked the boy his name and where he'd come from. At first the boy was relieved, and then he was angry. How could the policeman not have recognized him. He would grow up to bring the village its first measure of notoriety. His grandmother had lived in the village her whole life. It was a village set high in the mountains. The policeman carried the boy in his arms all the way home. At first the boy was relieved, and then he was angry.

28

There was no more mystery to solve, but there was a memory. Something on the tip of his tongue. Something that he'd wanted to say all along. He would have to recite the whole thing over again, exactly the way his grandmother had instructed him to.

Then for no particular reason, he looked up. The building had been under construction for a long time. Maybe construction was not the right word. Maybe reconstruction or reconfiguration was a more appropriate way of thinking about it. A personal decision to look up would not have been notable under any other circumstance, but he'd had the distinct impression that someone was looking at him.

It was a time before the war. He was young then, and very excited about the rapid advancement of his career. All the young men were very aggressive then, bustling between one superior's office and the other, constantly jockeying for position. It had all seemed so easy, so effortless, a time, seemingly, without end. When he'd first arrived in the capital, he had been well prepared for what he would face. It had all seemed so effortless.

He wanted to say that the past was better than the present, but that would have been too easy. Still, the phrase continued to haunt him. Then, for a split second, everything was different, and he felt as though he were turning into another person.

The boy sat on a hollowed-out log and buried his face in his hands.

His grandmother had forbidden him to enter the forest alone. His grandmother's cottage was near a road that led to the village in one direction and to the forest in the other direction. His grandmother had raised him single-handedly. He used to think about the stories his grandmother told him while he walked along the road that led to the lake. The lake was set high in the mountains. One day on his way to the lake, he saw a road he'd never seen before. The road appeared to run parallel to the road he was on. Another boy who appeared to be about his age stood on the parallel road. The boy on the parallel road waved to him. But when he waved back, the boy ran away. Frustrated, he sat on a hollowed-out log and buried his face in his hands. A policeman emerged from the forest. The policeman stopped in front of him and asked him his name and where he'd come from. The policeman gathered the boy in his arms and tried to comfort him. At first the boy was relieved, and then he was angry.

He would grow up to give the village its first measure of notoriety.

The policeman carried the boy all the way home in his arms.

One story was about a hunter who had disappeared from his family for a significant length of time. The hunter was thought dead. The family lived in a house with a great front window that led directly into the living room. One evening the hunter returned, and when he returned, he entered the house through a great front window.

The hunter took one giant step and returned to his house, returned home, through an open window.

$(p+r)^n$

Harold Abramowitz is a writer and editor from Los Angeles. His books and chapbooks include *Sin is To Celebration* (co-author, House Press, 2009), *Dear Dearly Departed* (Palm Press, 2008), *Sunday, or A Summer's Day* (PS Books, 2008), and *Three Column Table* (Insert Press, 2007). Harold co-edits the short-form literary press eohippus labs (www.eohippuslabs.com), and co-curates the experimental cabaret event series, Late Night Snack (www.latenightsnacks.blogspot.com).

Teresa Carmody is the author of *Your Spiritual Suit of Armor by Katherine Anne* (Woodland Editions, 2009), *Eye Hole Adore* (PS Books, 2008), and *Requiem* (Les Figues Press, 2005). She is the co-director of Les Figues Press.

Located in London having drifted from Belgium, **VD Collective** is a front (for Discreet Ventures in art DIY). Generally it stands for Variable Device and, in this instance, for Visual Duct. Vincent Dachy acts as the spokesperson of VD collective (vdachy@talktalk.net) and has had some *Tribulations* published by Les Figues Press.

TRENCHART Series of Literature

TRENCHART is an annual series of new literature published by Les Figues Press. Each series includes five books situated within a larger discussion of contemporary literary art; each title also includes a work of contemporary visual art in response to the book's text. All participants write an aesthetic essay or poetics; the first title in each series is the collection of these aesthetics, specially-bound in a limited-edition book available to subscribing members.

TRENCHART: Maneuvers Series

TrenchArt : Maneuvers
aesthetics

Sonnet 56
Paul Hoover

Not Blessed
Harold Abramowitz

The Evolutionary Revolution
Lily Hoang

The New Poetics
Mathew Timmons

Maneuvers Series Visual Artist: VD Collective

Become a subscribing member of Les Figues and receive all five titles in the TrenchArt Maneuvers Series.

LES FIGUES PRESS TITLES ARE AVAILABLE THROUGH:

Les Figues Press <http://www.lesfigues.com>
Small Press Distribution <http://www.spdbooks.org>

ƒ

LES FIGUES PRESS
Post Office Box 7736
Los Angeles, CA 90007
www.lesfigues.com
www.lesfigues.blogspot.com